W9-DAF-741

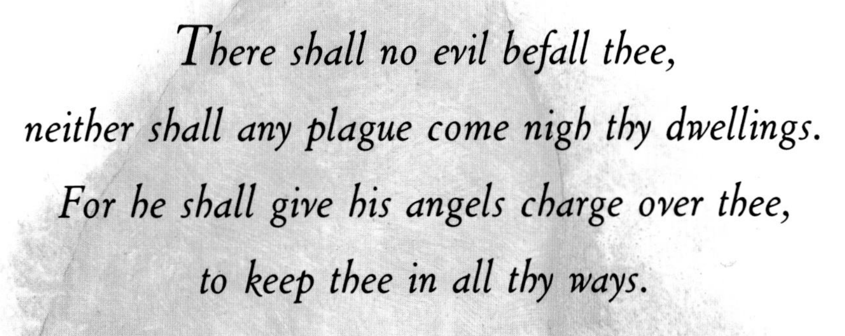

There shall no evil befall thee,
neither shall any plague come nigh thy dwellings.
For he shall give his angels charge over thee,
to keep thee in all thy ways.

PSALM 91:10, 11

NAOMI JUDD'S

Guardian Angels

performed by The Judds

illustrated by Dan Andreasen

HarperCollins*Publishers*

*This book is dedicated to all the family storytellers—relatives like my own aunts—
Toddie, Ramona, and Evelyn Judd, who link us together in a chain of dynastic awareness
and bring the past to life by giving voice to the ones who are now silent. Before there
were video cameras, tape recorders, or even photographs, the family storytellers gave
us our sense of where we come from so we can better plan where we want to be going.
Storytellers entertain, inspire, and comfort, as they connect us together in a web of belonging.*

—N.J.

For Sam

—D.A

FOREWORD

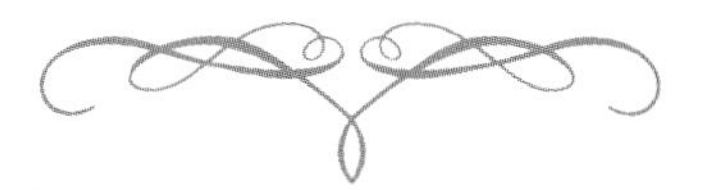

DO YOU BELIEVE IN GUARDIAN ANGELS? I surely do. Since I was a child, I've had the unmistakable sensation of being lovingly watched over, protected, and guided by one of God's celestial messengers. She's so real, I've named my Guardian Angel Elizabeth. So far I've even found over three hundred verses in the Bible referring to Guardian Angels.

One day a songwriter friend inquired about a group photo of my Judd ancestors taken at our original family homestead in Louisa, Kentucky, around 1900. As I described the lives of Elijah and Fanny Judd, my great-great-grandparents, and pointed out my grandfather, Ogden, at their knee, I spontaneously added, "If you'll look real close, you'll see our eyes are all the same." *Voilà!* A song was born. My favorite aspect of country music is the connection it brings all of us as it tells us about the lives of real folks.

As I brought Fanny and Elijah's personalities and their stories back to life, this song touched their descendents in ways that I could not have dreamed. Wynonna and Ashley said they appreciated the security of knowing their roots, and it made them more aware of their own accountability to our family. We did a Judd genealogy, and Wynonna even named her firstborn son Elijah. One of the greatest gifts any parent can give a child is roots and wings.

A hundred-year-old photograph stares out from a frame.

HOME
SWEET
HOME

And if you look real close you'll see
our eyes are just the same.

I never met them face-to-face
but I still know them well

from the stories my dear grandma would tell.

Elijah was a farmer
he knew how to make things grow.
And Fanny vowed she'd follow him
wherever he did go.

As things turned out, they never left their small Kentucky farm, but he kept her fed and she kept him warm.

They're my Guardian Angels
and I know they can see,
every step I take they're watching over me.

I might not know where I'm going
but I'm sure where I come from.
They're my Guardian Angels
and I'm their special one.

Sometimes when I'm tired
I feel Elijah take my arm.

He says keep a-goin',
hard work never did a body harm.

DIANA'S
ROOM

And when I'm really troubled
and I don't know what to do,

Fanny whispers, “Just do your best,
we’re awful proud of you.”

They're my Guardian Angels
and I know they can see,

every step I take they're watching over me.

I might not know where I'm going
but I'm sure where I come from.

They're my Guardian Angels
and I'm their special one.

A hundred-year-old photograph
stares out from the frame.
And if you look real close you'll
see our eyes are just the same.

A portion of the royalties received from the sale of this book shall benefit
The Judd Family Foundation, Inc., a Tennessee not-for-profit corporation.

Printed in China

Library of Congress Cataloging-in-Publication Data
Judd, Naomi.
Naomi Judd's Guardian angels / written and performed by Naomi Judd ; illustrated by Dan Andreasen.
p. cm.
Summary: A young girl looks at a picture of her great-grandparents and knows that they are angels watching over her.
ISBN 0-06-027208-2
1. Children's songs—United States—Texts. [1. Grandparents—Songs and music. 2. Songs.]
I. Andreasen, Dan, ill. II. Title
PZ8.3.J84Gu 2000 99-13676
782.42164'0268—dc21 CIP

Typography by Elynn Cohen
1 2 3 4 5 6 7 8 9 10
❖
First Edition
http://www.harperchildrens.com